By Jennifer Gray and Amanda Swift

GUINEA PIGS ONLINE

GUINEA PIGS ONLINE: FURRY TOWERS

GUINEA PIGS ONLINE: VIKING VICTORY

GUINEA PIGS ONLINE: CHRISTMAS QUEST

GUINEA PIGS ONLINE: BUNNY TROUBLE

GUINEA PIGS ONLINE: THE ICE FACTOR

PUPPIES ONLINE: TREASURE HUNT

Puppies Online

Puffin Patrol

Jennifer Gray & Amanda Swift

with illustrations by Steven Lenton

Quercus

For Archie
J.G.

For Carol, Gus and Harry
A.S.

For my nephew, Zak
S.L.

First published in Great Britain in 2015 by

Quercus Publishing Ltd
Carmelite House
50 Victoria Embankment
London EC4Y 0DZ

An Hachette UK company

A CIP catalogue reference for this book is available
from the British Library

ISBN 978 1 84866 520 0
EBOOK ISBN 978 1 84866 828 7

1 3 5 7 9 10 8 6 4 2

Printed and bound in Great Britain by Clays Ltd, St Ives plc.

Contents

1
Welcome Back!

On a sunny day in spring, Einstein, a little brown dachshund puppy, sat on the back seat of his owner's little car. The car was stuck in a traffic jam. Einstein looked up their location on his owner's tablet computer. '*Traffic jam*,' he read. I can see the evidence of that, he thought, looking out of the window at the long line of cars ahead and behind. He scratched his ear. But what I want to know is what's *caused* this traffic jam.

Not far behind Einstein's car, a big, fluffy, grey and white Old English sheepdog named Puzzle was peering out of the front window of his owner's smart grey saloon. Perhaps there's been in incident on the road ahead, he thought. Maybe a puppy's been kidnapped?

A little way behind that, a black and white, medium-sized springer

spaniel called Bounce leaned out of
the window of her owner's muddy
white jeep and sniffed the salty sea air.
I hope we get there soon, she thought.
So that I can get out and run around
and have fun!

All three puppies were on their
way to spend their holidays at Sandcliff
Lighthouse Kennels. They had been
there once before and had such an
exciting and fun holiday together.
They couldn't wait to return!

The long line of traffic crawled through the seaside village, along the road by the beach. Eventually the cars containing the three puppies squeezed through the traffic jam, climbed the narrow track up the hillside and pulled up outside the lighthouse.

The puppies jumped out. They were surprised to hear the sound of barking. New kennels had been put up in the garden! Inside the kennels were all sorts of other dogs that the puppies had never seen before.

The puppies greeted each other warmly. Puzzle gave Einstein and

Bounce a lick on the nose. Bounce leaped and barked. And Einstein held out his paw for the other two to shake.

'What's going on?' asked Puzzle. 'I thought it was going to be just us three staying here again this time.'

'You thought, but you didn't *know*,' said Einstein. 'You had no evidence that it would be just us three here again this time.'

Puzzle shook his shaggy head in disbelief. 'I see you're still droning on like a scientist,' he said. 'I thought you might be a bit more fun this holiday.'

'Don't worry about that,' said Bounce, doing little jumps over Einstein as if Einstein were a cone in a dog-training session, 'because *I'm*

even more fun than I was last time.
I've learned to juggle *and* I can
balance a ball on my nose.'

'What's the use of that?' asked
Einstein.

'You never know,' said Bounce.
'One day I might join a seaside
circus.'

Just then a girl of about nine
came out of the lighthouse. She wore
a T-shirt, shorts and sandals, and
she was smiling. The three puppies
immediately raced up to her.

'Jackie!' they cried, but of course
all she heard was barking.

'Hello, puppics!'
said Jackie, hugging
them all at once.
'How lovely it is to
see you again!'

Just then Jackie's
grandad Trevor,
the ex-lighthouse
keeper and current
owner of the
kennels, came out
to say hello.

'Welcome, welcome,' he said,
shaking the owners' hands and giving
the puppies a pat. 'Sorry if you got

held up in traffic. The beach has been closed this morning, for some reason. I don't know why.'

'Come and meet the other dogs, puppies,' said Jackie. 'Grandad built some new kennels. He only finished them last week and we're full already!'

'I hope none of them is sharing our bedroom,' said Puzzle. 'I'm not happy sleeping next to someone I don't know. They might bite me in the night.'

'I don't mind sharing our room, but it won't leave much space to play,' said Bounce.

'Let's wait and see what happens,' said Einstein.

They didn't have to wait long, because Jackie called them again to follow her.

'Heel!' she said. The puppies immediately did as they were asked.

Jackie looked impressed. 'Wow!' she said. 'You've really grown up in the last few months.' She led the way to the lighthouse. 'You three are in your old room. We didn't think it was fair for you to have to share, so the other dogs are all in the new kennels. We've made it really nice for them, with comfy baskets and toys, just like you've got.'

Einstein, Puzzle and Bounce raced up the stairs to their bedroom on the second floor of the lighthouse. Then they slid straight back down on the helter-skelter slide that ran around the inside wall. They did this a few times before they decided to stop and unearth all the toys in the box in their bedroom. Once Jackie was sure they were settled she went down to the kitchen to help make the tea.

'Ah, it's good to be back,' said
Einstein, trying out his soft round basket.

'We've got some new toys!' said
Bounce, still digging through the toy
basket. 'Wow! Little plastic balls! I can
use these to practise my juggling.'

'Never mind juggling, let's check
out the den.' Puzzle was staring at
the wooden stairs that led from the
bedroom to the old control room of
the lighthouse. On their last holiday
the puppies had used the control room
as a den. It was a secret meeting place
where they could make plans and go
on the computer.

'I wonder if there's a criminal hiding up there,' said Puzzle.

Einstein sighed. 'Are you still on about criminals? We looked last time, remember, and there wasn't.'

'I know, but one might have moved in since we left,' said Puzzle. 'You have to understand the criminal mind.'

'And you have to understand that I'm trying to have a nap.'

'I'm too excited to sleep,' said Bounce, bouncing up the wooden stairs. 'Come on, you two! Let's go up to the den and make some plans for our holiday.'

Puzzle and Einstein followed
Bounce. When she reached the top of
the stairs she carefully pushed open the
trapdoor to the control room.

'Don't forget to ask for the
password!' Puzzle called up.

'OK,' said Bounce. 'What's the password, Puzzle?'

'I can't remember,' said Puzzle.

'It's "pow-cat",' said Bounce.

'No it's not,' said Einstein.

'I remember now,' said Puzzle. 'It's "cat-pow".'

'It's not that either,' said Einstein. 'It's "cowpat". Now can we just stop talking and get up there?'

Bounce climbed up into the control room, followed by Puzzle. Then they both helped Einstein up because his legs were too short to climb up on his own.

'Wow! I'd forgotten how good the view is from here,' said Bounce, jumping up on to the swivel chair and looking out of the big round windows at the sparkling sea.

'Ah! It's good to be back,' said Einstein, checking out the computer and all the rest of the machinery.

'Right! How are we going to solve the crime?' said Puzzle, grabbing the binoculars.

'There hasn't been a crime,' said Einstein.

'Well, what are we going to do then?' said Puzzle.

'Let's go for a swim,' Bounce suggested.

'I can't swim, remember?' Einstein said.

'All right then, we'll teach you,' Puzzle said to him.

'Good idea!' said Bounce. 'And once you've got the hang of swimming I can teach you to juggle.'

'I see two problems with that plan,' said Einstein. 'Problem number one: I don't want my collar to get wet.' Einstein had a very special collar with a camera hidden in it and the camera would break if it got wet. 'Problem number two: I'm scared of the sea.'

'I can solve problem number one,' said Puzzle. 'You can take your collar-cam off!'

'And I can solve problem number two,' said Bounce. 'We'll teach you in the paddling pool!'

'But I don't even know which stroke to do!' said Einstein, sounding a bit panicky.

'That's easy,' said Bounce. 'Doggy-paddle!'

2
No Puffins

Einstein dipped a toe in the paddling pool. 'It's freezing! I'm not getting in there!'

'You are if I push you,' Puzzle said, edging towards him and giving him a shove.

'Stop it!' Einstein bounced off the side of the paddling pool.

'Honestly, it's fun! Look!' Bounce dived in.

SPLASH!

Drops of water showered over Puzzle and Einstein.

'I think I'll join you!' Puzzle panted. He took a run up.

'Wait until I take my collar off, can't you!' Einstein cried. Very carefully he slipped his collar-cam over his head and hid it under a bush.

SPLOOSH! Puzzle landed in the water.

This time a deluge of cold water engulfed Einstein.

'You might as well get in now,' Bounce said. 'You're wet through anyway.'

Einstein sighed. 'All right.' He clambered over the side of the paddling pool. Some of the air had gone out of it when Puzzle had landed. It sagged and wobbled like an old beanbag.

'Hurry up!' Bounce said.

'I'm trying!' Einstein slipped and slithered. Eventually he did a sort of somersault and landed on his bottom in the water.

'This is how you do doggy-paddle,' Bounce said. She circled her front paws, making a delicate splash.

Einstein copied her. 'I think I'm getting the hang of it!' he said.

'Only because you're sitting down,' Puzzle objected. 'Try it with your back paws off the ground.'

'I can't.' Einstein stood up. 'The water's too shallow.'

There were only about ten centimetres of water left in the paddling pool. It came up to Einstein's tummy.

'How did that happen?' Puzzle asked. 'I'll bet a criminal sneaked up and stole the water when we weren't looking.'

Einstein shook his head. Water dripped off his ears. 'There's a perfectly logical explanation. When *you* jumped in, the water was pushed out. It's called the Archimedes' principle.'

'Arky who?'

'Never mind.'

'There you are, puppies!' The puppies looked round. It was Jackie! She was with her friend Bradley. 'We thought you might like to take a trip over to the island in the boat.'

The island! The puppies glanced at one another. The island was where Mike Dodger lived. *Why would Jackie want to go there?* Mike Dodger was the local villain. He didn't like the puppies, or Jackie and Bradley for that matter. Last time the puppies stayed at the lighthouse they had stopped Mike from stealing some valuable treasure. Mike had ended up in a lot of trouble.

Einstein let out a curious yip.

Jackie seemed to understand. 'Don't worry, we won't go anywhere near Mike's house. We want to see the puffins. Grandad says they come every year at the same time to nest on the island.'

'Hooray!' Bounce leaped out of

the paddling pool. 'I've always wanted to see a puffin! What is a puffin by the way?'

'It's a seabird with a colourful beak,' Einstein told her. 'And how do you know you want to see one if you don't know what it is?'

'I just do!' Bounce said. 'I want to see everything. I love it here so much.'

The three puppies clambered out of the paddling pool. Einstein collected his collar-cam and slipped it back on.

'Let's go,' said Bradley. He threw his backpack over his shoulders. 'I've brought some biscuits in case we get hungry.'

'We'll have to take the boat,' said Jackie. 'The tide's covering the causeway.'

The causeway was a path from the mainland to the island but at high tide it was covered by water.

The children led the way along the cliff path towards the beach where the boat was pulled up on to the sand.

The puppies trotted after them.

'You do realize what this means, don't you?' Puzzle said.

'What?' Bounce chased about, pretending to catch rabbits.

'We can look for clues.'

'What sort of clues?' puffed Einstein. His legs were so short he was struggling to keep up.

'Clues about what Mike Dodger's up to.'

'We don't know he's up to anything,' Einstein said.

'That's why we have to look for clues!'

'That's not logical.'

'Yes it is.'

'No it isn't.'

'Stop arguing,' Bounce said. 'Come and chase rabbits instead. It's way more fun.'

Puzzle charged after her but Einstein didn't have the puff. Luckily Jackie noticed he had dropped behind. She picked him up and gave him a kiss on the nose.

'Silly Einstein,' she said. 'If you didn't spend so much time barking, you wouldn't get so tired.'

Einstein snuggled into her. He couldn't argue with that!

*   *   *

'Are you sure this is the place?' Bradley asked.

The boat bobbed about in the water.

'I think so,' Jackie said.

'But there aren't any puffins,' Bradley said.

The puppies scanned the island

carefully. The boat was in a safe spot near the beach. Away to their right was Mike's house. To their left the land rose up from the sea in a grassy headland.

'They should be over there,' Jackie said, pointing towards the headland.

'Maybe we should take a closer look,' Bradley suggested.

'OK.'

He and Jackie jumped out and pulled the boat on to the sand. The puppies followed – quietly this time. They didn't want to alert Mike Dodger. And they sensed that something was wrong.

The little group set off towards the headland.

'Grandad said the puffins make their nests in burrows,' Jackie said. 'That's why they like it here. I don't understand where they've gone.'

She flopped down on to the grass

with Bradley. They unpacked the backpack. Bradley had brought two lots of biscuits: some chocolate digestives for him and Jackie and some dog biscuits in the shape of bones for the puppies.

'I'm starving!' Puzzle went and sat beside the children. He gave Jackie a pleading look with his big eyes and laid his chin on her knee.

'You can have one in a minute, Puzzle,' Jackie laughed.

'Why don't you take some photos?' Bradley suggested to her. 'So that we can show your grandad.'

Jackie took her mobile phone out of the backpack. She held it up and took some snaps of the deserted hillside.

'Where do you think the puffins have gone?' Bounce whispered to Einstein.

Einstein sniffed about. There were lots of old puffin burrows but they were all empty. 'Search me. Something must have frightened them away,' he said.

'I told you Mike Dodger was up to something,' Puzzle said without looking round. He was still concentrating firmly on the biscuits.

'We don't definitely know it's because of Mike—' Einstein began.

'We don't definitely know it isn't,' Puzzle shot back.

'Here we are.' Jackie opened the packet of dog biscuits.

'CA-HA-HA! CA-HA-HA! CA-HA-HA!' A horrible cawing came from somewhere above them.

'What's that noise?' Bounce whispered.

The puppies looked up. So did the children.

'Look out!' shouted Bradley. 'It's a seagull!'

An enormous grey and white bird hurtled towards them out of the sky. It snatched the packet of dog biscuits out of Jackie's hand and flew off.

'Give them back!' Bounce set off in pursuit but the seagull flew on to a rock where she couldn't reach it.

'CA-HA-HA! CA-HA-HA! CA-HA-HA!' it cawed, tearing into the biscuit packet with its sharp beak.

'Are you all right?' Bradley asked Jackie.

'I think so!' Jackie smiled bravely. 'And anyway I'm not going to let that horrible bird spoil our fun.' She carefully unwrapped the cellophane on the digestives. 'Just this once, you can have one of these instead!' She gave one each to the puppies.

The puppies wolfed the biscuits down.

'Now come here,' Jackie said. 'I'll take a selfie.'

'What's that?' asked Einstein.

'I know,' said Bounce. 'It's when you take a photo of yourself on a phone. My owner does it all the time so she can show me the exciting places she's been to.' Bounce's owner was a stuntwoman. She travelled all over the world.

'Oh, OK,' Einstein said. He straightened his collar.

The two children knelt down with

the three puppies in front of them.
Everyone crowded into the picture.

'Smile!' said Jackie. She pressed the
button. 'Let's do another one with the
puppies on our laps,' she said.

They did that too.

'Now let's get one of the puppies
on their own!'

'This is fun!' Einstein barked.

Very soon the puppies were having
such a lovely time making silly faces
for the photos that they
forgot all about
the annoying
seagull.

3
Poo Alert!

'Look!' said Jackie. 'No puffins.'

The next morning Jackie was showing Trevor the photos she'd taken of the empty hillside. They were sitting outside the lighthouse on deckchairs while all the dogs played in the garden.

'Nopuffins!' said Bounce. 'Let me see!'

She rushed over to Jackie and rested her head on Jackie's arm so that she could see the photos. Einstein and Puzzle followed their bouncy friend.

'I can't see them,' said Bounce.

'That's because they're not there,' said Puzzle.

'But Jackie said there were "nopuffins". I want to see if they look different from puffins.'

Einstein sighed. 'There's no such thing as a "nopuffin". Jackie just means there AREN'T ANY PUFFINS. No offence, Bounce, but sometimes you are quite silly.'

Bounce turned away from Jackie and hung her head. Einstein could see that he had made her feel sad. He tried to cheer her up.

'But you're good at lots of things,' he said to her.

'Like what?' asked Bounce.

'Like . . . swimming!' said Einstein. 'Could you give me another lesson?'

'Of course I could!' said Bounce. She jumped up and rushed over to the paddling pool. Einstein followed her.

'I'll stay here and listen for clues,' said Puzzle. 'I'm good at that.' And he sat very still with his head cocked to

one side because he thought that being
good at listening meant not just actually
being good at listening but *looking*
like he was good at listening.

'We've had puffins here every year since I've been here,' Puzzle heard Trevor say to Jackie.

'So why do you think they haven't come this year?' Jackie asked.

'I don't know,' replied Trevor. 'The only reason I can think of is that the sea is too dirty for them to fish.'

'But there's a blue flag on the beach! That means the sea is really clean.'

'I know,' said Trevor. 'It's a puzzle.'

Puzzle rushed over to the paddling pool.

'It's a puzzle!' he said to Bounce and Einstein.

'What is?' said Bounce.

'That there are no puffins!'

'Is that all you've found out?' asked Einstein.

'Well, what have you done while I've been over there?' asked Puzzle.

'I've been working on my stroke,' said Einstein.

'He has,' said Bounce. 'Show Puzzle what you can do.'

Einstein made little digging movements with his paws. Bounce and Puzzle watched.

'Not bad,' said Puzzle. 'I think you're ready to try it when there's water in the paddling pool.'

Just then Jackie came over with some brand-new bright yellow tennis balls.

'Playtime!' she called. All the dogs rushed over to her, wagging their tails. Jackie threw one of the balls as hard as she could and the dogs raced after it, apart from Einstein, who tried to measure the speed of the ball by calculating the distance it travelled and the time it took. He did this because he was scientific, but also because he was rather slow, and he didn't want to be the last to get to the ball.

Jackie watched the ball travel through the air. Then she saw Mrs Bossy marching towards the lighthouse. Mrs Bossy was Bradley's gran. She was a tall, thin woman with half-moon spectacles and hair piled up on top of her head in a bun. She lived in a pretty cottage beside the beach. The problem was she didn't like dogs. And she was very bossy.

The ball was travelling towards Mrs Bossy and so were all the dogs chasing it.

'Look out, Mrs Bossy!' Jackie cried.

Mrs Bossy paid no attention. The ball landed on her head and got stuck in her hair. Bounce was the first to reach Mrs Bossy. She and all the other dogs jumped up at her, trying to get the ball.

Mrs Bossy was furious.

'Get these disobedient dogs off me!'
she shouted.

'They're not disobedient,' Jackie
protested. 'They're just excited.'

'Well, calm them down!' Mrs Bossy shouted back.

Jackie whistled loudly and straight away all the dogs stopped jumping up at Mrs Bossy, turned round, went back to Jackie and sat at her feet.

Jackie patted their heads. 'Good dogs,' she said.

Mrs Bossy marched over to Jackie and Trevor. She stood in front of them. Then she got the local newspaper out of her handbag and thrust it into Trevor's hands.

'For me?' he said. 'Thank you, Mrs Bossy. I like to keep up with the local news.'

'You need to do more than keep up, Trevor. You need to be shut down.'

'But the puppies only jumped up! They didn't hurt you,' said Jackie.

'It's not about that, it's about the beach. It's covered in dog poo! Look!'

The puppies crowded round Trevor's deckchair so they could see.

Mrs Bossy pointed to a big photo of Mike Dodger. He looked just as weird as ever with his enormous wig, puffy coat and platform shoes. He was pushing a machine that looked like a cross between a Hoover and a giant poop scoop.

THE SANDCLIFF TIMES
Local Hero Saves Beach!

'Local hero?' Bounce barked. 'That doesn't sound right.'

'Shhh! Listen!' hissed Einstein.

'Sandcliff Beach had to be closed yesterday thanks to you,' Mrs Bossy snapped.

'Me?' exclaimed Trevor. 'What do you mean?'

'It was covered in dog poo,' Mrs Bossy said. 'It must have been the dogs at your kennels: you've got so many now. The council had to hire Mike Dodger and his Poover to clear up the mess.'

'A Poover? What on earth is that?' asked Jackie.

'It hoovers up poo,' snapped Mrs Bossy. 'It's fantastic, but it's expensive. And the council can't afford to keep paying for it, which means that there has to be a stop to poo on the beach. And that means there has to be a stop to your kennels. I've told the council to shut you down.'

'But—' Trevor said.

'No buts. We have to keep our blue Clean Beach Flag. If we lose it, no one will come to the beach. And that will be the end of Sandcliff.'

Mrs Bossy turned round and walked straight back down the hill. Then she realized she hadn't taken the ball out of her hair so she put her hand to her head, found it and chucked it over her shoulder. It fell to the ground. This time none of the dogs ran after it. They didn't feel like playing any more.

'This calls for a meeting,' said
Einstein to Puzzle and Bounce.

'In the den in five minutes,' said
Puzzle.

'I've forgotten the password. Is it
"cowpat"?' said Bounce.

'Bounce!' said Einstein. 'You're not
supposed to say it in front of all the
other dogs!'

'They're not listening,' said Bounce,
looking over at the other dogs. They

werc crowded round Trevor, who had a plastic bone in his hand.

'I was,' said a cheeky-looking Labrador pup.

'So was I,' said a scary-looking Alsatian.

'Now we'll have to change it,' said Puzzle.

The three puppies went into the lighthouse.

'OK,' said Einstein. 'It needs to be something that's easy to remember,'

'Yes,' said Bounce. 'How about "dog poo"?'

4
The Case of the Smelly Beach

Up in the den the puppies had a meeting.

Einstein took charge. He switched on the computer and jumped up into the swivel chair to look at the screen.

'The Case of the Smelly Beach,' he declared. 'First of all we need to make a list of our key suspects.'

'Mike Dodger,' Bounce and Puzzle said together.

Einstein tapped the name out on the keyboard. 'Who else?' he asked.

The two puppies looked blank.

'It's obviously him,' said Puzzle. 'We know he's a crook.'

'Maybe,' said Einstein, 'but that doesn't mean he definitely did it. We still have to prove it scientifically.'

'How?' asked Puzzle.

'The first thing to do is to eliminate everyone else from the enquiry,' Einstein said importantly.

'What?' asked Bounce.

'Show that it couldn't have been anyone apart from Mike,' Einstein explained.

'Oh, I get it,' said Bounce. 'You mean like me, for instance?'

'Yes,' said Einstein. 'Good thinking, Bounce. We'll start with you. Where were you when the poo appeared on the beach yesterday morning?'

'I was in the car, on my way here,' Bounce said. 'I didn't go to the beach at all except when we went to get the boat with Jackie and Bradley. And that was afterwards.'

'Excellent, so we know it wasn't you.' Einstein had typed Bounce's name. Now he deleted it. 'Puzzle?'

'It definitely wasn't me,' said Puzzle. 'I've got an alibi.' He said this word very proudly because it was something he'd learned from his owner, who was a detective.

'Is that a type of flea?' Bounce said, edging away from him.

'No, it means that someone was with me when the crime was being committed.'

'Oh,' said Bounce, 'who was that?'

'My owner!' He gave her an affectionate nudge. 'I was in the car like you!'

'Oh yes!' Bounce wagged her tail. 'I think I'm getting the hang of this detective business.'

'Now it's my turn to ask questions,' said Puzzle. 'What about you, Einstein? Do you have an alibi?'

Einstein sighed. 'I was in the car with *my* owner, you dummy!'

'I'm not a dummy. You're
the one who said we had
to eliminate everyone
from the enquiry!'
Puzzle retorted.

'I was just trying
to explain things to
Bounce—'

'What about the other dogs at the
kennels?' Bounce interrupted. 'Mrs
Bossy thinks it was them. They could
have done it before we arrived.'

'I knew those dogs were acting
suspiciously as soon as I saw them,'
Puzzle growled.

'No you didn't,' said Einstein.

'Yes I did!'

'No you didn't.'

Bounce held up a paw. 'Shhh. You're giving me a headache. And my brain's working very hard here trying to be a detective.'

'It can't be the dogs from the kennels,' Einstein said, 'because Jackie and Trevor always clear up the poop with a scoop and put it in bags in the red bin. I've seen them. So even if Trevor did take them down to the beach he wouldn't have left any mess. And anyway,' he added, 'Jackie's right;

the dogs are very well behaved. Did you see the way they came to heel when she called them just now?'

Even Puzzle couldn't disagree with that. 'So that leaves Mike Dodger,' he said. 'I told you!' Then he narrowed his eyes. 'The question is, *why*?'

'Why what?' Bounce asked.

'Why did Mike Dodger cover the beach in dog poo?' Puzzle said. 'My owner says criminals always have a motive for committing crime. Usually it's because they want to take over the world, or get revenge on someone who was mean to them in the past . . .'

'Or because they want money!' Einstein added. 'I think you're on to something, Puzzle.'

'I am?' asked Puzzle in surprise.

'Yes. Don't you remember? Mrs Bossy said the council was paying Mike to clean up the beach with the Poover and that it was very expensive!' Einstein tapped away at the keyboard. 'Let's have another look at that newspaper report online.'

Bounce and Puzzle stood on their hind legs either side of the swivel chair with their front paws up on the counter so that they could see the screen.

LOCAL HERO SAVES BEACH

Local hero, Mike Dodger, came to the rescue yesterday when resident Mrs Edith Bossy woke to discover that beautiful Sandcliff Beach had been covered with dog poo overnight. Mrs Bossy, whose cottage fronts the beach, was shocked at what she saw.

'It was everywhere!' she said. 'I've never seen anything so disgusting in my life. It's since all those dogs arrived at Sandcliff Lighthouse Kennels. If you want my opinion, that place should be closed down before this happens again!'

Luckily, Mike – who lives a stone's throw away on nearby Mike's Island – was on hand to help out with his brilliant new invention, the Poover, which sucks up poo in an instant, leaving the beach clean and fresh once again.

A spokesman for the local council said: 'It was very fortunate that Mike was able to help with the clean-up operation at such short notice. Of course we had to pay him two thousand pounds to do the job, but it was worth every penny to keep our blue Clean Beach Flag. Well done, Mike! Meanwhile, our Health and Safety team will look into claims that Trevor Trumble, owner of the Sandcliff Lighthouse Kennels, is responsible for the dirty beach.'

'Two thousand pounds!' Bounce whistled. 'How many dog biscuits could you buy for that?'

'A lot,' said Einstein, 'although the exact number would depend on which variety you bought.'

'So what are we waiting for?' Puzzle said. 'Let's go and arrest him.'

'We can't,' said Einstein. 'We don't have any proof.'

'So what do we do now?' asked Bounce.

'We know *why* he covered the beach in dog poo,' said Einstein. 'We just need to find out *how*. Then we can take the evidence to Jackie and Trevor, and save the kennels. We'll sneak over to the island first thing tomorrow on the causeway when the tide's out and take a look around.' He tapped his collar-cam with his paw. 'We'll take pictures of anything we find with this.'

The puppies all agreed this was a very good plan. They also agreed that all that detective work had made them very hungry and that it must be time for lunch.

5
Filthy Rich!

As soon as Bounce woke up the next morning she looked at the clock in the puppies' bedroom. The little hand was just past the seven so that must mean it was just past seven o'clock, but the big hand was on the three so that must mean it was three o'clock! She couldn't decide which was right so she looked out of the window. It *looked*

like it was morning so she decided to
wake the others up. She went over to
Einstein and licked his face.

'Time to get up!' she whispered.
'What time is it?' asked Einstein.
'It's time to get up,' said Bounce.

'Sounds like you don't know what time it is.'

'I do. It's either seven o'clock or three o'clock.'

Einstein opened an eye and looked at the clock.

'It's quarter past seven. The little hand tells you the hour. The big hand tells you the minutes. So when the little hand is on the seven and the big hand is on the three that means it's seven fifteen.'

'But when the *little* hand is on the three it means it's three?' asked Bounce.

'Yes.'

'Oh, I get it!' Bounce said. 'So numbers can mean different things at different times?'

'I suppose so,' said Einstein. He was beginning to feel quite confused himself!

'Because that would explain why sometimes I'm full up after one biscuit and sometimes I feel like I could eat twenty-five.'

Einstein didn't answer. He had fallen back asleep. Bounce sighed and went over to Puzzle. She gave him a lick on the face.

'It's morning!' she whispered,

rather than trying to tell him the time. She wanted to get on with their day.

'So it is!' said Puzzle, immediately wide awake. 'It's time to investigate Mike's Island!'

Puzzle and Bounce woke Einstein again and the three puppies slid quietly down the slide and crept out of the lighthouse without waking Trevor or Jackie. Then they tiptoed past the kennels where the other dogs were sleeping and made their way down to the sea below the lighthouse. When they got to the seashore they were disappointed to see that the water

came right up to the rocks. There was
no way they could walk across the
causeway to Mike's Island.

'Drat! It's high tide,' said Einstein.

'Why are you surprised? Isn't it always high tide in the early morning? It was last holiday,' said Bounce.

'Yes, but the tides vary. It's not always high tide or low tide at the same time. It depends on the sun and the moon.'

'The moon?' said Bounce. 'I can't see the moon.'

'That doesn't make any difference,' said Einstein. 'It has an effect even when you can't see it. It's all to do with gravitational forces.'

Bounce sighed. 'We're meant to be

on holiday, but you make me feel like I'm at school.'

'I can't help it,' said Einstein. 'My owner is always explaining things to me.'

'I guess that's because she's an Archimedes,' said Bounce.

'You mean archaeologist,' said Einstein.

'Well, I'd like someone to explain something to me. How are we going to get over to the island?' asked Puzzle.

'We could swim,' said Einstein.

Bounce and Puzzle looked at Einstein in surprise.

'I thought you were scared of the sea,' said Puzzle.

'I was. But I've been eating too many biscuits and I could do with the exercise,' said Einstein.

'I think you might need another lesson first,' said Bounce.

'OK,' said Einstein.

'All right then,' said Puzzle, 'why don't we go to the beach now? It's easier getting in the sea where there's sand rather than pebbles, and it's shallower. Then when we've given Einstein another swimming lesson we can go to the island at low tide.'

The three puppies set off and were soon overlooking the vast stretch of soft white sand.

'Doesn't it look lovely?' said Bounce.

'Yes, and there's not a poo in sight,' said Puzzle.

'Let's hope it stays that way,'

said Einstein. He led the way to
the water's edge. Then he lowered
his head to take his collar-cam off.
While he was hiding it under a rock,
something soggy landed nearby.

'Yuck!' he squealed. 'What was
that? It stinks.'

'Yuck!'

'Yuck!'

Puzzle and Bounce had also narrowly avoided being hit on the head by something brown and smelly.

'It's dog poo!' yelped Einstein. 'And it's coming from over there!'

The three puppies looked out to the sea. A hail of dog poo was being fired over the water. Most of it landed on the beach but some of it fell straight into the sea.

The puppies ran for cover. They threw themselves behind a pile of deckchairs. Then they peeped round to see what was going on.

'It's being fired from the island!' said Puzzle.

'Look at the beach now! It looks all brown and messy, like it did in the newspaper!' said Bounce. 'And the sea's all dirty!'

'This must be the work of Mike Dodger,' said Puzzle. 'He's firing dog poo at the beach so that he can make lots of money cleaning it up with the Poover.'

'Look!' said Bounce. 'There he is!'

An inflatable dinghy was coming towards them across the sea. In it sat Mike Dodger and his Poover. And on top of Mike's wig sat the seagull they had seen on the island.

'That's the bird who stole our biscuits!' said Einstein.

'What's it doing with Mike?' asked Bounce.

'Spying, I suspect,' said Puzzle.

As the dinghy neared the shore the puppies shrank back behind the pile of deckchairs. They watched as Mike Dodger hopped out of the dinghy and pulled it on to the beach.

'Ha ha!' said Mike, wheeling the Poover on to the dirty sand. 'I'll soon be rich! Filthy rich! And no one will ever find out the stinking truth that I'm responsible for the poo! Go and wake up Mrs Bossy, Art,' he shouted up to the seagull.

The seagull took off.

'CA-HA-HA! CA-HA-HA!' the

seagull screamed as it flew over to
Mrs Bossy's cottage.

Very soon Mrs Bossy
appeared on the doorstep in
her nightie. 'What's going on?'
she called.

'It's only me, Mrs B,' Mike
called back. 'I just thought I'd
let you know the poo's back.
I've got to clean up again
this morning.'

Mrs Bossy stared at the dirty beach
in disgust. 'Right,' she said. 'That's it.
I'm going to ring the council again
about those kennels.'

She went inside. Mike set about poovering the beach. The seagull gobbled up all the crusts of bread and soggy chips from the litter bins.

When Mike finished poovering the beach he called to the seagull, 'Come on, Art, let's get out of here. We'll take the bag of poo out of the Poover, plop the poo back in the tank for tomorrow and get some breakfast.'

Mike Dodger got into the dinghy and sped back towards the island. The seagull flew after him.

When the coast was clear the puppies crept out from behind the deckchairs.

'What does he mean, plop it back in the tank for tomorrow?' said Bounce.

'He's recycling it,' said Einstein, 'but not in a good way. He's going to fire it at the beach again.'

'Maybe that's why the puffins have gone,' Bounce said all of a sudden, 'because Mike's making the sea round the island all pooey.'

'Gosh, Bounce, I think you might be right!' Einstein said.

'We've got to stop him,' said Puzzle. 'Or the puffins won't come back.'

'And nor will we,' said Einstein, 'because the kennels will be closed down!'

6
The Poo Plot

After breakfast the puppies waited anxiously by the paddling pool. The tide was nearly out. Now was their opportunity to cross the causeway to Mike's Island.

'Let's just go!' Puzzle said.

'We can't,' Einstein objected. 'What if Jackie and Trevor see us?'

'They won't see *me*,' said Bounce,

'because I'll be so fast I'll just look like a blur. And they won't see *you*, Einstein, because you're so small.'

'They'll see me though,' Puzzle said.

'Either way they'll wonder where we've gone,' said Einstein, 'and send out a search party.'

Just then Jackie came out of the lighthouse with Trevor. They were carrying empty shopping bags.

'Are all the dogs safely locked up in the kennels?' Trevor asked his granddaughter. 'I don't want them going down to the beach when we're out.'

'It's OK, Grandad,' Jackie replied.

'They're all inside, except for the puppies. I thought they could come with us to the shops and choose some more dog biscuits. That horrible seagull ate our last packet.'

The puppies glanced at one another in dismay. Normally they would have loved a trip to the shops to buy dog biscuits, but that would mean they couldn't carry out their mission on the island.

'We've got to persuade Jackie to let us stay here!' Einstein whispered.

'How do we do that?' Bounce asked.

'Pretend to be asleep!' suggested Puzzle.

The three puppies flopped down beside the paddling pool and closed their eyes.

'You know, Jackie,' came Trevor's puzzled voice, 'I'm sure it wasn't our dogs who made all that mess on the beach. But I simply can't understand how it got there.' He sighed. 'Not that it matters much, everyone blames the

kennels anyway. I've just had Mrs
Bossy on the phone again. Apparently
there was more poo on the beach
this morning. I'm really worried she'll
force the council to close us down.'

'Don't worry, Grandad,' Jackie
replied. 'Mrs Bossy can't do anything
unless she has proof that we're
responsible. And we're not!'

'You're right,' said Trevor,
sounding more cheerful. 'Come on,
I'll buy you an ice cream.' The
puppies heard him close the door of
the lighthouse.

'Hurry up, puppies,' Jackie called

over to them. 'We're going to the shops.'

'Don't move!' hissed Einstein.

The puppies didn't budge. Puzzle let out a big snore.

Einstein opened one eye, then closed it very quickly. Trevor and Jackie had come over and were peering down at them.

'They look done in,' Trevor observed. 'Anyone would think they've been up for hours.'

If only he knew! thought Einstein.

'Maybe we should leave them here,' Jackie suggested. 'They can't escape if we close the gate.'

Puzzle let out another big snore.

'All right,' Trevor agreed. 'Just this once.'

'See you later, puppies!' Jackie called back. 'Don't get up to any mischief while we're out. Don't go anywhere near the beach and if Mrs Bossy comes, hide!'

Jackie and Trevor got into the car and slammed the doors.

Einstein opened one eye, then

the other. He watched the car drive off along the narrow road. 'They've gone!' he said. 'You can get up now.'

'Hooray! Now we can go to Mike's Island.' Bounce was on her four paws before Einstein had finished speaking. 'Let's go!'

Puzzle let out another big snore.

'You can stop pretending now, Puzzle,' Einstein said.

'I don't think he is pretending,' Bounce said. 'He really is asleep!'

'Oh, for goodness' sake!' Einstein said.

'Don't worry, I know what to do.'

Bounce jumped in the paddling pool.
Then she jumped out again and shook
herself. Droplets of water sprayed all
over the other two puppies.

'Be careful of my collar-cam!'
Einstein yelped.

Puzzle had woken up. 'You're
not wearing it. You took it off at the
beach, remember?'

'Oh no!' Einstein gasped. 'I left it under a rock.'

'We'll have to get it later,' said Bounce firmly. 'Otherwise we won't have time to go to Mike's Island and investigate.'

'OK,' Einstein agreed. 'But let's make it quick. I need to find my collar-cam before my owner discovers it's missing.'

'How are we going to get out of here?' Puzzle asked, inspecting the chain on the garden gate.

'We'll go under the fence,' said Bounce. 'I dug a hole yesterday so I could chase the rabbits.'

The puppies scampered after Bounce. They slipped under the fence and scrambled down to the sea. Cautiously they began to cross the causeway towards the island.

'We'd better watch out for that seagull,' Einstein said.

'I'll go ahead and check that the coast is clear,' offered Bounce. She raced ahead.

Einstein trotted after her as quickly as he could and Puzzle brought up the rear. Neither of them said anything. Einstein was still fretting about his collar-cam and Puzzle was dreaming about the biscuits Jackie and Trevor had gone to the shops to buy.

Very soon they reached Mike's Island. The causeway ended in a path that led through a garden up the hill to Mike's front door.

Bounce rushed up. 'All clear,' she

said. 'There's no sign of Mike or that rotten seagull.'

'What's that awful noise?' asked Einstein, sitting down and putting his paws over his ears.

Loud music was coming from the house through an open window. It was accompanied by a dreadful wailing.

'Mike's singing, I think,' said Bounce. She frowned. 'Or it might be the seagull. It's hard to tell.'

'Maybe it's a duet,' said Einstein.

'What are those?' Puzzle waved a paw at three cylindrical black metal objects mounted on concrete blocks on the lawn. They had holes at one end, which pointed out to sea towards Sandcliff Beach.

'I think I know . . .' Einstein was about to tell him when Bounce spoke.

'They're cannons,' she said.

Einstein looked at her in amazement. 'How did you know

that?' he asked. 'Have you been studying history?'

'No,' Bounce replied cheerfully. 'My owner sometimes gets fired out of them when she does stunts.'

Puzzle went up and poked his head into the open end of the first cannon. 'Yuk!' he said, withdrawing it again immediately. 'Are they always this smelly?'

'They are if they've recently been used to fire dog poo,' Einstein said, twitching his nose.

'You mean Mike's using the cannons to get the poo on to Sandcliff Beach?' Bounce exclaimed.

Einstein nodded.

Puzzle whistled. 'You've got to admit that man is a criminal mastermind!'

'If he's so good at being a criminal, how can we stop him?' asked Bounce in despair.

'We've got to get inside his head,' Puzzle said, pacing about like he'd seen detectives do on TV shows.

'Inside his *shed*, you mean,' Einstein said. 'Look.' He pointed a paw at the back of the concrete blocks. A thick plastic pipe ran along the grass behind them. Three smaller pipes led from it into the back of each cannon. The other end of the thick pipe was concealed inside a large wooden shed.

The puppies tiptoed up to the door of the shed.

Puzzle pushed the door open with his paw. The three puppies edged in.

Inside the shed there was lots of machinery. It clanged and clunked and whistled and hummed noisily.

Einstein inspected the machinery. He pointed to a tank. 'The poo is in there,' he declared.

'Are you sure?' asked Puzzle.

'Yes. That's where the plastic pipe from the cannons ends up.'

'And look!' said Bounce excitedly. 'Here's the switch to fire the poo!'

Attached to the tank was a dial. The dial had three settings: OFF, ON and FULL BLAST! It was currently switched to OFF.

'We need my collar-cam,' said Einstein. 'Then we can take a video to show Jackie.' He turned towards the door. 'We'll have to come back tomorrow when we've got it.'

'But that will be too late!' said Bounce. 'There must be something we can do now!'

Just then there was a horrible squawking outside the shed.

'Oh no!' whispered Bounce. 'It's the seagull.'

'Art,' a voice shouted from the direction of the house. 'Can you turn on the hot water? I need a bath. I stink from poovering up that disgusting dog mess.'

The seagull let out another volley of squawking. The door creaked open.

'It's coming in here!' hissed Puzzle.

'Now what are we going to do?' Bounce squeaked.

Bounce and Puzzle looked at Einstein expectantly.

'Hide!' he ordered.

7
Bath Time
(for Mike)

'CA-HA-HA, CA-HA-HA!' cawed
the seagull. It flew towards a second
tank, which stood in the corner of the
shed.

'That must be the hot water,'
whispered Einstein.

Then, suddenly and without
warning, Bounce leaped out from
behind the poo tank where the puppies

were hiding. She grabbed the seagull in her jaws, stunning it. It lay in a daze in her soft mouth.

'Bounce,' said Einstein, 'you have just acted foolishly for two reasons. One, the seagull has now seen us and could inform Mike Dodger that we are trespassing on his property and, two, you don't eat birds, remember? Last time we were given chicken at the kennels you didn't eat it because you said your owner has chickens and it's not fair to eat someone you live with.'

Bounce dropped the seagull to the

floor and then pounced on it with two paws so it couldn't get away.

'I wasn't going to eat it,' she said. 'Anyway, I can't help catching birds. I'm a hunting dog. I'm trained to do it.'

'CA-HA-HA, CA-HA-HA,' cawed the seagull. It began to struggle.

Bounce sat on its tummy.

The seagull eyed them nastily.

Just then Mike Dodger called out from the house. 'Where's that hot water, Art? I've got to get rid of this stink!'

'We'd better turn it on,' said Bounce, 'so he doesn't suspect anything.'

Puzzle went over to the hot-water tank and put his paw on the switch. He was about to flick it on when Einstein held out a paw to stop him.

'Wait!' said Einstein. 'I've had an idea. Let's give Mike Dodger a little surprise at bathtime. And I don't mean a plastic duck! Let's spoil his bath the way he's spoiled the sea for the puffins.'

'That's a brilliant idea, Einstein. How do we do it?' said Puzzle.

'Simple. We unscrew the poo pipe. Then we unscrew the water pipe.

Finally, we screw the poo pipe into the water tank.'

'Got it!' said Puzzle, and he quickly did exactly as Einstein had said, while Einstein watched to check Puzzle was doing it right and Bounce stayed sitting on the seagull.

'Done!' said Puzzle when he had finished.

'Good,' said Einstein. 'Now turn on the hot water.'

Puzzle flicked the switch.

'Let's see if it works,' said Einstein. He darted out of the shed door and over to the house. The door was open, so Einstein slipped in. Puzzle followed and Bounce bounded after him, closing the shed door carefully behind her so that the seagull couldn't escape.

The puppies crept upstairs. They peeped round the bathroom door to see what Mike Dodger was doing.

'Hurry up and heat up!' moaned Mike Dodger.

He was sitting in his bath wearing his coat and platform shoes. Clearly he thought it saved time to wash his clothes and his body together. But he wasn't wearing his wig. It sat in front of him in the bath on a wig stand.

'He obviously likes to look at his hair while he's washing it,' Puzzle remarked to the others.

'What's happened to this hot water?' grumbled Mike Dodger as he turned the taps on as far as they would go.

There was a gurgling and a glugging in the pipes and then, without warning, a huge jet of liquid poo shot out of the taps.

'Aaaargh!' Mike screamed. He leaped out of the bath before the poo could hit him, but he was too late to save his wig. The poo splashed on to it and changed its colour from shiny black to dirty brown.

'Elvis!' cried Mike Dodger. 'You're ruined!'

'Who's Elvis?' whispered Bounce to Einstein.

'His wig,' Einstein whispered back.

'Do humans always name their wigs?' asked Bounce.

'Only when they love them as much as Mike Dodger loves his,' said Einstein.

Mike Dodger grabbed a bottle of bubble bath and tipped it over Elvis. Poo was still pouring out of the taps.

'I don't believe this!' cried Mike Dodger. 'Why is poo coming out of the taps?'

'Because we recycled it into your

bath!' said Puzzle quietly from behind the door and the three puppies giggled softly.

Mike desperately tried to turn the taps off but in his confused state he turned them on full. The poo poured out with even more force.

'Elvis! Don't leave me!' cried Mike.

Elvis was drowning in poo. Mike turned the taps the other way. Now they were off but it was too late for Elvis. Mike grabbed another bottle of bubble bath (he was given ten bottles every Christmas by his ten aunties) and poured it all over the wig. It dripped off and went down the plughole. The room began to smell of lavender and roses, with a hint of dog poo.

'Mission accomplished,' said Einstein.

'But there's poo everywhere,' said Bounce.

'Yes, but there's also bubble bath going down the drain,' said Einstein. 'That will disperse the poo. It'll end up in the sewers like the water from the toilet.'

'So Mike Dodger won't have any poo left to fire on to the beach?' said Puzzle.

'Exactly,' said Einstein. 'And there won't be any more falling in the sea, which means the puffins might come back.'

'And we can go and see them and have some more biscuits,' said Bounce, 'without that horrid seagull stealing them again!'

8
Pooper Snoopers

The next morning the puppies were outside playing by the paddling pool. Bounce and Puzzle were giving Einstein another swimming lesson.

'Go on, Einstein – you're nearly there!' Bounce yelled in encouragement.

'Paddle!' shouted Puzzle.

Einstein paddled furiously. Then he reached out and touched the side of the

paddling pool with his paw. 'I did it!'
he proclaimed proudly. 'A whole lap
without touching the bottom!'

'Well done!' Bounce gave
Einstein's wet nose a lick. 'I think
you're ready to swim in the sea now.'

'Then I can get my collar-cam back too,' said Einstein. 'I hope I can remember which rock it's under. I wish we hadn't left it there for a whole day.'

'I'll help you look, Einstein,' said Bounce. 'We've been so busy with Mike and the poo business we haven't had a chance to go and get it.'

'Let's get a quick photo before we go,' Puzzle said. 'I'll go and find Jackie.'

He raced back towards the lighthouse. Very soon he reappeared, tugging Jackie by her trouser leg.

'I'll be back in a minute,
Grandad,' Jackie called behind her.
'I think Puzzle wants to show me
something.'

'All right then, I'll make a start on
the washing up. And when we're done

we'll take all the dogs for a walk to the beach,' Trevor called back.

'Trevor seems much happier today,' Bounce remarked.

'That's because there's no dog poo on the beach,' said Einstein. 'Which means the kennels won't have to close down.'

'Oh yes!' Bounce said. 'I'd forgotten about that.'

Einstein frowned. 'How could you have forgotten about it already? We only solved the crime yesterday.'

'Because I like thinking about nice things instead of dog poo,' said

Bounce. 'Like chasing rabbits.' She looked up. 'Talking of which . . .' She shot off across the lawn.

Puzzle let go of Jackie's trouser leg and bounded over to the paddling pool. 'Do it again!' he told Einstein, 'while Jackie's looking.'

'OK.' Einstein set off once more to do another lap of the paddling pool.

'You can swim, Einstein!' Jackie exclaimed. 'Let's get one quick selfie all together with Einstein in the middle,' she said, 'so I can send it to Bradley. Then I'd better go and help

Grandad.' She pulled out her phone. The puppies posed for the photo.

Just then Bradley peddled up on his bike.

'Great timing!' said Jackie. 'Now you can be in the selfie as well. Einstein's learned to swim,' she told him while they all crowded into shot.

'Well done, Einstein!' Bradley scratched the little dachsund between the ears. 'I'm so pleased Gran doesn't have anything to complain about today,' he said to Jackie. 'I knew that poo on the beach wasn't anything to do with the kennels, but you know what Gran's like when she gets an idea into her head.'

'It's all right,' Jackie reassured him. 'I know you didn't blame us.' She paused. 'I wonder how it got there though. I mean, if it wasn't the dogs at the kennels, where did it come from? Someone must have done it deliberately.'

'But why would anyone do such a horrible thing?' Bradley shook his head. 'It's a complete mystery.'

The puppies glanced at one another.

'If only we could tell the kids what

really happened,' Einstein said.

'Well, it doesn't matter now,' said Bounce.

'It might,' said Puzzle gloomily.

'How come?' asked Einstein.

'Because Mike's still at large. He's liable to reoffend at any minute,' said Puzzle in his detective voice.

'What's he talking about?' Bounce asked Einstein.

'He means Mike might do it again.'

'But how can he?' asked Bounce. 'He got rid of all the dog poo with bubble bath.'

'Don't forget we're dealing with a criminal mastermind,' Puzzle said. 'He could strike at any place, any time.'

The sound of a loud engine interrupted their musings. A van zoomed up the track to the lighthouse and skidded to a halt beside the red dog-poo bin.

'Who's that?' asked Bradley.

'Search me,' Jackie replied.

A man got out of the van and tottered towards the bin. He wore a baseball cap and a yellow reflector vest with the logo *Sandcliff Council Pooper Scooper* written on the back in marker pen.

'He must be from the council, I guess,' Jackie said. She looked puzzled though. 'I wonder why he's come today.'

'What do you mean?'

'Well, the rubbish collectors normally empty the dog-waste bin on Friday and today's Thursday.' She shook her head. 'And I've never seen them in a jacket like that: normally they just wear overalls.'

'I smell a rat,' whispered Einstein.

'I think it's dog poo you can smell, not rat,' said Puzzle, sniffing deeply.

'No!' Einstein snapped. 'I mean there's something fishy here.'

'It's definitely not fish.' Bounce wrinkled her nose. 'I'd say Puzzle's right. It's dog poo. It's coming from the red bin.'

'Stop being so silly!' snapped Einstein. 'What I mean is there's something suspicious going on. Look at his feet!'

Three pairs of keen eyes followed the man as he put the last of the poop bags into the back of his van.

'Einstein's right!' barked Bounce. 'He's wearing platform shoes!'

'And a puffy coat!' exclaimed Puzzle.

'And a cap instead of a wig to disguise the fact that he's bald,' said Einstein.

'It's Mike Dodger,' Bounce cried.

'He's stealing more poo!'

'I told you he'd strike again!' said Puzzle. 'Quick! We need to tell Jackie and Bradley it's him!' He ran towards Mike, barking loudly.

Bounce and Einstein followed.

'What's the matter with the puppies?' asked Bradley.

'They don't like that man from the council,' replied Jackie. She tried to call them off, but the puppies wouldn't come.

'Get these mangy mutts away from me!' shouted Mike Dodger, kicking at the puppies.

'Wait a minute,' said Jackie. 'I recognize that voice. It's Mike Dodger!'

Just then Trevor came out of the lighthouse. 'Mike?' he said. 'What are you doing here? And where's Elvis?'

'Elvis?' Jackie echoed. 'Who's Elvis?'

'Mike's wig,' chuckled Trevor. 'He's named his wigs all sorts of things over the years, haven't you, Mike?

Dolly, Elizabeth, Elton – the latest one is Elvis.'

'Elvis had a little accident, Trev,' Mike said. 'I had to bury him in the garden.'

'Oh, I'm sorry to hear that,' Trevor said.

'Why are you emptying the dog-poo bin?' Jackie demanded.

'Because I've got a new contract with the council to dispose of the poo,' Mike snapped back.

'Since when?' asked Bradley.

'Er . . . none of your business,' said Mike.

'Make sure you dispose of it properly, Mike,' Trevor frowned. 'Because Jackie and Bradley took the boat out the other day to look for puffins but there weren't any to be seen. Puffins won't fish where it's dirty, you know, which means they won't nest either.'

'I don't care a bag of dog diarrhoea about puffins,' Mike retorted rudely. 'All I care about is cash. And if I don't get this lot in the van before too long I'm not going to make any. Now get these horrible puppies out of the way before I squash them.'

He got into the van and zoomed off.

'*Now* what are we going to do?' asked Bounce. 'We can't tell the humans about the cannons . . .'

'. . . or how Mike's going to use the dog poo from the bin to fire at the beach so that he can clean up with his Poover,' said Puzzle.

'We'll have to rely on their intelligence,' said Einstein. 'Don't worry, they're almost as clever as dogs. They'll work it out.'

The three humans were watching Mike's van disappear along the narrow track.

'Grandad,' Jackie said slowly, 'you don't think Mike's got anything to do with the dog poo on the beach, do you? I mean if all he cares about is cash and he's making a lot of money poovering it up, maybe he's responsible for putting it there in the first place.'

'See?' whispered Einstein.

'I wouldn't put it past him,' Trevor sighed. 'He's always been a troublemaker.'

'But how does he get the poo on to the beach without being seen?' Bradley wondered.

Trevor shrugged. 'Goodness knows.' He went back into the lighthouse. 'I'll call the council and tell them Mike's behaving suspiciously. With any luck they'll send the coastguard over to the island to investigate. Then I'll finish the washing up and take the dogs for a walk. You two go and have some fun with the puppies.'

'What if they don't send the coastguard?' Jackie said to Bradley in a low voice. 'What if Mike puts more poo on the beach and Mrs Bossy blames Grandad? He might really get closed down if it happens again.'

'There's only one thing to do,' said Bradley. 'We'll have to go to the island and get proof Mike's responsible for the dirty beach.'

Jackie's eyes shone. 'I was hoping you were going to say that,' she said. 'Come on, puppies, let's get the boat.'

9
Stop the Plop

Before the boat had even touched the
jetty on Mike's island, Bounce had
jumped out and swum to the land. She
was followed by Puzzle and then, to
the others' amazement, by Einstein.
But although he paddled as hard as
he could with his little paws, he didn't
move forward in the water because
the current was pulling him back.

'Einstein!' Jackie called in alarm. She tried to reach out to him, but the boat was too far away. Puzzle and Bounce watched from the jetty with worried expressions.

'He's not going to make it!' said Puzzle.

Bounce charged back into the water.

'He'll be cross if you help him,' Puzzle called to Bounce.

'I'd rather he be cross than at the bottom of the sea!' Bounce called back, just before she gently took the scruff of Einstein's neck in her jaw and pulled him ashore, where she dropped him safely on the land.

Einstein shook himself dry and then said to Bounce, 'What did you do that for? I was trying to swim.'

'See?' said Puzzle to Bounce. 'I told you he'd be cross.'

'Well, next time he tries to swim, remind me not to save his life,' said Bounce, shaking herself next to Einstein so that he got wet again.

Einstein understood that he'd annoyed Bounce. And for once he decided he should apologize.

'Sorry, Bounce,' he said. 'Thanks for helping me.'

And he licked her on the leg. He would have licked her on the nose but he couldn't reach.

'That's OK,' said Bounce.

As soon as Jackie and Bradley had tied up the boat the puppies raced up the hill to Mike Dodger's shed. Jackie and Bradley followed them.

'How come they know where to go?' asked Bradley.

'Perhaps they've heard something,' said Jackie.

But when they got near the shed Jackie changed her mind. 'I don't think it's something they've heard. It's something they've smelled!'

The smell of poo was so bad that both children held their noses while the puppies leaped at the door of the shed.

Jackie put her hand on the handle

and started to turn it.

'I wish they'd hurry up,' said Einstein. 'If *they* find the smell bad, can't they imagine how *we* find it?'

'At times like this, I wish our sense of smell wasn't that brilliant. In fact, I wouldn't mind having a cold so I couldn't smell anything at all,' said Bounce.

Bradley put his hand on Jackie's. 'What if Mike Dodger's in there?'

The two children each put an ear to the door.

'I can only hear a machine noise,' said Jackie.

'Me too,' said Bradley. 'Let's go in.'

Jackie turned the handle and slowly opened the shed door. She, Bradley and the three puppies peered round it.

There was no one in the shed, but the tank was whirring as it churned up the poo, ready to send it down the pipes. Jackie and Bradley walked round the tank and saw the pipes that led from the tank to the shed wall. Then they looked out of the window and saw that the pipes led from the shed to the three black cannons outside.

'So it is him!' said Bradley. 'We were right. And now we've got proof that Mike Dodger is behind the poo plot.'

'Would you believe it? He's set all this up,' said Jackie, 'so he can fire poo at the beach and make money clearing it all up!' She pointed at the Poover, which was parked in the shed beside the poo tank.

'I don't know why they're telling us things we already know,' said Bounce.

'They're telling each other,' said Puzzle.

'But *they* already know what they're telling each other,' said Bounce. 'Why don't they hurry up and do something? Mike Dodger might be here in a minute.'

'They're thinking before they act,' said Einstein. 'You should try it some time.'

'I just did!' Bounce went up to Jackie and nudged her back pocket.

Jackie looked bewildered. 'What is it, Bounce? I don't have any biscuits on me.' She patted her pocket. Then she smiled. 'My phone! Good idea, Bounce. I'll take photos as evidence.'

Jackie had only taken a few snaps
when they heard the sound of a bird
cawing.

'CA-HA-HA! CA-HA-HA!'

'Oh no!' said Bounce. 'It's that
horrible seagull again! You know,
Mike's friend – Art. It must have seen
us. Now it's going to tell Mike.'

But before the puppies
could warn Jackie and
Bradley, the door to
the shed was opened
wide and Mike
strode in, wearing
a huge blond wig.

'Get off my property, you nosy brats!' shouted Mike.

'We're not being nosy, we're just looking for the truth,' said Jackie bravely. She put her phone back in her pocket to hide it. 'And now that we've found it, we can go and tell everyone that Mike Dodger isn't a hero after all.'

While Jackie was talking, Einstein hopped onto the Poover and stood on his hind legs. He gently slipped the phone out of her back pocket with his teeth.

'What are you doing?' hissed Puzzle.

'Wait and see!' Einstein got the phone into position with his paws, being careful not to let Mike Dodger see him. 'You two protect Jackie and Bradley. They might need some help.'

'OK.' Puzzle and Bounce focused their attention on Mike.

Jackie moved towards the door and Bradley followed her.

Mike Dodger stood in their path. 'You're not going anywhere!'

Puzzle and Bounce began to growl.

'Please could you stand aside, Mike?' said Bradley.

'I am not Mike,' said Mike. 'I am Mike's twin brother, Ike.'

'OK, Ike,' said Bradley, playing along. 'Perhaps you could pass on a message to Mike. Tell him he's in trouble. He's responsible for polluting Sandcliff Beach.'

'I'm not!' shouted Mike Dodger, ripping off the blond wig to reveal his bald head. 'I'm cleaning the poo off the beach! I'm providing a service!'

'Keep growling,' Einstein whispered to his friends.

Puzzle and Bounce carried on growling.

'Yes, but then you're firing it back on the beach,' said Bradley.

'And then I'm clearing it up again.'

'And then you're being paid a huge amount of money by the council,' said Jackie.

'Yes, I am!' said Mike. 'And that makes me rich. And I deserve to be rich because I work really hard.'

'That isn't work,' said Jackie. 'It's crime.'

'She's good, isn't she?' said Puzzle.

'I wish we had it on film,' said Bounce, as Einstein slipped the phone back into Jackie's pocket.

'We have,' said Einstein. 'And so does everyone else.'

Before Puzzle and Bounce had a chance to ask Einstein any questions Mike Dodger opened the shed door.

'I'm not going to stand here and listen to you calling me a criminal.'

He charged off across the lawn and the puppies chased after him, barking. Mike ran full tilt across the pipes that led from the shed to the

cannons. The puppies followed. Mike
was gaining ground, but when he
got to the last pipe his platform shoe
tripped on the metal and he fell on to
his hands and knees.

The puppies caught up with him.
Bounce opened her jaw and grabbed
Mike's coat. She held tightly on to it
so that he couldn't move.

'Get off me!' Mike spluttered. 'This is my island and I do what I want on it!'

He quickly unfastened the poppers on his jacket and slipped out of it. Before the puppies had a chance to grab him he got up and raced away from the pipes towards the sea.

'Fetch!' called Jackie as she and Bradley clambered over the pipes. While Bounce dropped the coat on the ground, Puzzle raced ahead after Mike.

'Hurry, Puzzle!' called Bradley.

Just as Puzzle reached him, Mike

changed direction and ran to one side. Puzzle skidded on the grass as he tried to turn at speed. Mike had got away!

'Get him, Bounce,' barked Puzzle.

Bounce tore after Mike and got close to him, but then Mike changed direction again! He was zig-zagging up and down the grass.

Einstein quickly worked out Mike's tactic and ran to face him. Mike laughed when he saw the little dog bounding towards him.

'You don't scare me, little sausage dog!'

'Don't you dare call me a sausage

dog!' growled Einstein and he lunged, but Mike turned round and ran in the opposite direction. As soon as he turned he saw Bounce poised to catch him. Mike turned again and started to run, but saw Puzzle crouching and waiting.

Mike was trapped, surrounded by puppies on all sides. Jackie and Bradley caught their breath as they watched.

'They're rounding him up!' Jackie exclaimed.

'Stay low!' Puzzle ordered Bounce and Einstein. 'And creep forward.'

'Puzzle's using his sheepdog skills!' said Bradley. 'He's rounding up Mike like a naughty sheep.'

The puppies crept forward. Mike looked all around him. He couldn't move.

'OK, I surrender,' said Mike with panic in his voice.

The puppies didn't answer. They just slowly moved forward, forcing Mike to move forward too.

'They're going towards the cannons!' Jackie said.

Mike was getting nearer and nearer the big black cannons. The puppies were getting nearer and nearer Mike. When they arrived at the cannon, Puzzle led the countdown.

'Three . . .'

Bounce knew what to do next.

'Two . . .'

Einstein knew what to do next.

'One!'

On the count of 'one' the puppies moved forward all together.

Mike backed away from them and grabbed the cannon.

The puppies growled.

'I said, I surrender,' Mike shouted. 'Now leave me alone!'

'We will,' said Bradley, 'but we haven't quite finished with you yet!'

Then the children rushed forward and tipped Mike head first into the cannon. He struggled and kicked his legs in the air but it didn't make any difference. He was well and truly stuck.

The puppies sat back and panted.
Their job was done.

'Well done, puppies!' said Jackie.
She and Bradley gave the puppies a big
hug.

Then they all heard clapping behind
them. The puppies and the children
looked round to see who it was. To
their amazement, they saw Trevor,
Mrs Bossy and the local police walking
towards them across Mike's lawn.

'Well done, all of you. Mike Dodger has been caught in the act.'

'Grandad! What are you doing here?' said Jackie.

'You sent me photos of you confronting Mike on my mobile.'

Jackie was surprised. She felt for her phone. It was in her pocket. She turned to Bradley. 'Did you take photos and send them to Grandad's phone?' she asked.

'No,' Bradley replied.

'Well, maybe the dogs did,' Trevor joked.

'Well, maybe they did,' said Jackie, but she wasn't joking.

She gave the puppies another hug. 'Let's get a selfie of all of us together,' she said.

'She treats those dogs as if they're her best friends,' said Mrs Bossy, shaking her head.

'They are,' said Trevor. 'And having friends is marvellous. Perhaps you should try it, Mrs Bossy?'

10
Clowns of the Sea

That evening Trevor was reading the
late edition of the local newspaper
while he ate his fish and chips. The
rest of the dogs had gone home in the
afternoon so it felt like back to normal
for the puppies with just the three of
them and Jackie and Trevor sitting
quietly together in the lighthouse's cosy
kitchen. The puppies felt a little sad that

they hadn't got to know the other dogs better after all. They had been so busy solving crime they hadn't had time to make friends properly. They decided they would try harder next time.

'Look at this, you three!' Trevor put the newspaper on the floor so that puppies could see the front page.

Underneath the headline was a copy of the selfie Jackie had taken just before Mike Dodger was arrested and taken away by the police.

The puppies moved closer to get a better look.

'I hope my owner doesn't see it,' said Einstein gloomily.

'You don't look that bad,' said Puzzle.

'I'm not worried about what I look like,' Einstein snapped. 'I'm worried she'll see I'm not wearing my collar-cam. She won't let me come here on holiday again if I've lost it.'

'We'll get it tomorrow,' said Puzzle. 'Jackie's bound to take us to the beach for a walk. It's our last day!'

'You have no reason to think that she will,' said Einstein. 'She might take us somewhere else. And even if she does take us to the beach, my collar-cam might not be there. Someone might have stolen it.'

'Great! Another crime to solve!' said Puzzle.

'It wouldn't be great,' retorted Einstein. 'It's my collar-cam we're talking about. What if it was your dog biscuits that were missing?'

'I see what you mean,' said Puzzle.

'I've got an idea,' said Bounce. 'Let's go and get it tonight when Jackie and Trevor are asleep.'

This was such a good idea that even Einstein couldn't think of anything wrong with it. 'OK,' was all he said.

Trevor chuckled. He'd been listening to the puppies' barks. 'If I didn't know any better, I'd say those puppies could talk!'

'Isn't it weird how humans don't actually realize we can do all the things they can?' Einstein remarked as they cuddled up on the couch next to Jackie.

'I can do *more* than they can,' said Puzzle.

'Like what?' asked Einstein.

'Like eat biscuits all day without being sick,' said Puzzle.

'I can balance a ball on my nose while I'm swimming,' Bounce said.

'And I can take photos with my collar-cam on an archaeological dig,' said Einstein, 'which is why we need to go to bed now so that we can get up at midnight and find it.'

'Can we have a midnight feast
too?' asked Bounce.

'Only if we find my collar-cam.'

'We'd better find it then,' said
Puzzle.

To Jackie's surprise the puppies got down off the couch and made their way upstairs to bed. 'See you in the morning,' she said to them. 'Sleep well.'

'I'll stay awake,' said Bounce when the puppies reached their bedroom. 'Then I don't have to worry about telling the time when I wake up.'

'That doesn't make any sense,' said Einstein. 'You can't tell the time even if you stay awake.'

'I could count it,' said Bounce.

'All right,' said Einstein. He thought for a moment. 'There are three thousand six hundred seconds in an hour,' he said, 'and three hours until midnight, which means wake us up when you count to ten thousand eight hundred.' He and Puzzle settled down to sleep.

Bounce lay down in her basket. It was harder counting time than she thought, especially after a busy day. Instead she counted rabbits. Then she counted squirrels. Then she counted puffins. Then she counted nopuffins . . .

'Bounce!' She felt a small paw shaking her shoulder. 'Wake up, it's one o'clock! You fell asleep!'

'Did I?' she said. 'It was the puffins' fault.'

'What puffins?' said Einstein.

Bounce looked blank.

'Oh, well never mind that now. Jackie and Trevor are asleep. It's time to go and find my collar-cam. Hurry!'

The puppies whizzed down the helter-skelter slide and crept out of the door. The moon was out and it bathed the beach in a yellowy light. They picked their way carefully along the cliff path.

'It's over here somewhere,' said
Einstein, sniffing about among the
rocks.

'CA-HA-HA! CA-HA-HA!' a
mournful voice called.

'What was that?' whispered
Bounce.

'I hope it's not that horrible seagull again,' said Puzzle.

'Found it!' Einstein trotted towards them with the collar in his mouth. He placed it carefully on the sand. 'Can someone hold it so I can put my head through?' he asked.

'I will.' Bounce went to pick it up.

Just then there was a flutter of wings. 'CA-HA-HA! CA-HA-HA!'

'Look out!' shouted Puzzle.

Art the seagull swooped. He grabbed the collar-cam in his beak, then took off again into the sky.

'He's got my collar-cam!' Einstein cried.

The three puppies watched Art circle above the lighthouse and glide downward towards the sea with the collar-cam in his beak.

'He's taken it to the rocks beneath the lighthouse!' said Bounce.

'We'll never find it there!' Einstein moaned.

'Yes we will,' said Puzzle, 'if we turn on the light.'

'Which light?' asked Bounce.

'The one in the den,' replied Puzzle. 'The big one that Trevor used in the old days to show the ships the way in the dark.'

'That's a brilliant idea, Puzzle,' said Einstein. 'Let's go.' He shot off back to the lighthouse.

'Gosh, look at Einstein!' Bounce shot after him. 'All that swimming seems to have done him good.'

Puzzle galloped along after them.
'Wait for me!'

Very soon they were back at the
lighthouse. The puppies madc a plan.

'I'll turn on the light,' said Einstein.

'I'll go after the collar-cam,' said
Bounce.

'And I'll get the biscuit tin for the
midnight feast,' said Puzzle.

The other two looked
at him sternly.

'Oh all
right, I'll help
Bounce first,'
he said.

'OK, give me a minute.' Einstein disappeared inside the lighthouse. Bounce and Puzzle heard the scratch-scratch of his little claws as he scampered up the stairs and a happy little yelp as he managed to jump up into the den. All the swimming practice had made him strong enough to do it by himself.

Not long after, a bright light lit up the sky. It shone across the sea and down on to the rocks.

'My turn,' said Bounce, springing into action. She climbed off the path and on to the steep rocks.

'Be careful,' said Puzzle. 'It might
be slippery.'

'Don't worry,' said Bounce,
jumping nimbly from one rock to the
next.

'Can you see it?' Puzzle called.

'Yes, it's just here. Art's made a nest. There are eggs in it as well.'

'You'd better watch out,' Puzzle warned. 'Art will be angry if he thinks you're stealing his eggs.'

'Art's not here,' said Bounce. She reached out a paw and hooked the collar-cam.

'CA-HA-HA! CA-HA-HA!'

'He's coming, Bounce!' shouted Puzzle. 'Hurry, before he sees you near the nest.'

Bounce clamped the collar-cam between her jaws and leaped from rock to rock in the direction of the path.

'CA-HA-HA! CA-HA-HA!' Art was visible now in the light. He flew at Bounce angrily.

Bounce ducked. She felt her back paws slide under her on the slimy rocks. She almost lost her balance. 'Help!' she cried, although it came out as 'ullllpppp' because she had Einstein's collar-cam in her mouth.

Art circled above, waiting to attack again.

'Hold on, Bounce,' shouted Puzzle. 'I've got an idea.' He raced back inside the lighthouse. Sitting on the table in the kitchen were some of the dog biscuits Jackie and Trevor had bought when they went shopping. Puzzle grabbed the packet in his mouth and rushed back outside. He dropped the packet on the ground beside the edge of the cliff. 'Here!' he shouted at Art. 'Take these if you're hungry. Leave Bounce alone! You can't eat a collar-cam anyway!'

'CA-HA-HA! CA-HA-HA!' Art swooped on the biscuits. Then he disappeared over the side of the cliff back to his nest.

'Phew!' Bounce struggled over the last of the rocks and back on to the path. She dropped the collar-cam on the ground and lay down on it in case Art returned. 'That was close!' she said. 'Thanks, Puzzle.'

'That's all right,' said Puzzle. 'I'm glad you're OK.' He sighed. 'Pity about the midnight feast though.'

Just then the light went out. Very soon Einstein rejoined them. 'I saw everything that happened,' he said, his little tail wagging. 'Thank you, Bounce. Thank you, Puzzle. You really are my best friends. If there's anything you ever need me to do for you, don't hesitate to ask.' He wriggled into his collar-cam.

'Can you teach me to tell the time?' Bounce asked him shyly.

'With pleasure,' Einstein agreed.

'Can you burrow into the kitchen cupboards to look for more biscuits?' Puzzle asked.

'Well,' Einstein began, 'I'm not sure I should . . .'

'I'm awfully hungry,' Puzzle added. 'And you did say if we needed anything we only had to ask and I really need a biscuit.'

'OK,' said Einstein. 'Just this once.'

★   ★   ★

'I should have known those naughty puppies were planning something when they went to bed early,' said Jackie to Bradley the next morning. 'They ate all the biscuits on the kitchen table AND all the biscuits in the cupboard.'

The children were preparing a

picnic. Trevor had
suggested they should
go for another trip
in the boat to Mike's
Island to see if the
puffins had returned.
The three puppies
hid behind the kitchen
door, spying.

'I should never have let you
talk me into stealing those biscuits,'
Einstein grumbled. 'Jackie might not
take us with her now.'

'I didn't talk you into anything,'
Puzzle said. 'You talked yourself into it

by promising to do anything I needed.'

'Oh I do hope she takes us,' said Bounce. 'I really, really want to see a puffin.'

'The puppies did help us solve the mystery of the poo on the beach though,' Bradley was saying. 'So you can't be too cross with them.'

'That's true,' Jackie agreed. She packed up some sandwiches and crisps in a backpack and put in a bottle of water and two cups. 'I'm not really cross,' she said, 'it's just that I don't have anything else to give them to eat on the picnic.'

'I might starve if there's no food!' said Puzzle. 'What if we get shipwrecked?'

'We can walk back on the causeway at the next low tide,' Einstein said. 'That's what.'

'There are some cold sausages,' said Bradley, opening the fridge. 'Can we take those for the puppies?'

'Yes, all right,' Jackie agreed. 'I don't think Grandad will mind. You wrap them in foil, I'll get the puppies' water bowl.'

The three puppies wagged their tails in delight. *Sausages!* They were even better than biscuits.

The little group set off to the beach. Soon they were speeding across the sea in Trevor's boat.

'Look!' cried Jackie. 'There's a puffin!'

A black and white bird with a curved colourful beak rose up into the sky from the headland. Then it tucked its wings into its body and dived into the sea.

'It's fishing!' said Bradley in delight. 'That means the sea is clean again.'

The puffin emerged from the water carrying a fish and flew back to the headland.

'There are loads of them!' said Jackie. 'Oh look, puppies! Aren't they beautiful?'

The puppies followed her gaze. Lined up in the tufts and ridges of the headland were hundreds and hundreds of puffins.

'Oh,' said Bounce, wagging her tail in delight. 'You were right, Einstein, they're way better than nopuffins.'

Bounce was so excited Einstein chose not to correct her this time. 'Did you know that puffins are called clowns of the sea,' he said instead, 'because of their beaks?'

'I didn't,' said Bounce, 'but I do now, which reminds me, I need to show Jackie my new circus tricks when I get to the beach.'

'And I need to practise my swimming,' said Einstein.

'And I need to eat sausages,' said Puzzle.

And that's exactly what they did. And they played and played until it was nearly time for their owners to collect them.

'We'll see each other next time,' said Bounce, as Jackie headed back towards the lighthouse, 'won't we?'

'We'll see each other before that,' said Einstein. He tapped his collar and winked. 'I've been videoing the whole time this afternoon. I'll send it to you as soon as I get home.'

'That'll be great,' said Bounce. 'But we won't have any film of you.'

'Yes you will,' said Einstein. 'I've taken some selfies.'

'Wow,' said Puzzle. 'Is there

anything you don't know how to do?'

'I'm not great at balancing a ball on my nose.'

'You will be,' said Bounce. 'We'll teach you on our next holiday.'

'But first we'll have to find a ball that's as small as your nose,' said Puzzle to Einstein.

'True,' said Bounce. 'That might take a long time.'

'Not as long as it'll take me to race you to the lighthouse,' said Einstein.

Einstein ran off as fast as he could. Puzzle and Bounce followed but soon overtook him. It didn't matter because before they got to the door they all leaped on each other and rolled on the grass, playing, like best friends do.

Don't miss even more puppy pandemonium in

Puppies Online
TREASURE HUNT

The woof-tastic trio has discovered an ancient treasure map . . . but so has the evil Mike Dodger! Can Puzzle, Einstein and Bounce use their super skills to sniff out the treasure first?

GET YOUR PAWS ON IT NOW!

Quercus

For special offers,
chapter samplers,
competitions
and more,
visit . . .

www.quercusbooks.co.uk
🐦 @quercuskids